A NET TO CATCH THE WIND

A NET TO CATCH THE WIND

BY MARGARET GREAVES

DRAWINGS BY
STEPHEN GAMMELL

HARPER & ROW, PUBLISHERS

NEW YORK • HAGERSTOWN • SAN FRANCISCO • LONDON

J
G

Library of Congress Cataloging in Publication Data
Greaves, Margaret.
   A net to catch the wind.

   SUMMARY: A princess shows her father the importance
of freedom and love when he tries to capture a silver
colt that is dear to her.
   [1. Unicorns—Fiction.   2. Princesses—Fiction]
I. Gammell, Stephen.   II. Title.
PZ7.G8Ne 1979   [E]   78–20265
ISBN 0–06–022104–6
ISBN 0–06–022105–4 lib. bdg.

• For Nick •
who knows the same forest

A NET TO CATCH THE WIND

It was high summer when Mirabelle first saw him. He was only a foal then, the color of gray moonlight, with a silver mane and tail.

She had slipped away from the palace into the deep forest beyond. Mirabelle loved the forest. It was cool and full of shadows and little shifting pools of sunlight. It was strange and secret, full of unknown things, magic things perhaps. It sheltered flocks of colored birds, and rabbits and squirrels and the big-eyed, delicate-footed deer. It breathed with the scent of flowers and the sound of running water, and at night it held all the stars in its branches.

The foal was grazing alone, fetlock deep in grass and flowers, in an open glade between the trees. He had not seen her. He was so beautiful that she hardly dared to breathe. Then the light wind took her scent toward him. He raised his head and lifted a curled foot, till with a startled whinny he swerved and galloped away.

"Oh, don't go!" she called after him. "I'd never hurt you. Please don't go."

Perhaps he heard her. As he reached the trees he turned and looked back. Dark and round and shining, his eyes met hers, shy yet friendly, as if he understood.

When she returned to the palace Mirabelle told her father, the King, about all the things she had heard and seen in the forest. But she never said anything about the moonlight-colored foal. Her father boasted that he had the most magnificent horses in the world, and he could never see a fine one without wanting to own it. Mirabelle felt that her foal should never be owned. He was free as cloud and sky and water. So she said nothing at all about him, though day after day she longed for him and looked for him. But she never again glimpsed a single hair of his silver-gray coat.

Summer flowed softly into autumn. The leaf-ripping wind shrilled through the forest, and autumn closed into winter. The King loved to ride in the brisk, cold air and often took his daughter with him. They were returning home one day with a company of riders, hurrying because of the weather. The first snow of the year had begun to fall, softly, steadily, smoothing and spreading itself over the branches as if all the bright birds of summer were settling in drifts of white feathers.

Suddenly, in an open glade, they saw him. He was older now, a colt with a coat like silver. His head was high, his flaring nostrils sniffing the unknown snow, ears back, and eyes huge with alarm. The King reined in, holding up his hand for silence.

"Have you ever seen a colt more beautiful?" he whispered. "I must have him. Catch him!"

But already the colt had whirled and fled, as if it had dissolved into the whirling flakes themselves.

"Leave him, Your Majesty," advised Magus. "His kind must always be free."

Magus was the oldest and wisest man at court. He was said to know hidden things and words of power, and the King would usually listen to him. But not today.

"I will have him," he repeated proudly. "This forest is mine and all things in it belong to me."

In their holes and burrows and nests the wild things of the forest heard, and each laughed in its own way. As if anyone could own *them*! But Mirabelle was frightened for the silver colt.

"Sire," protested Magus, "living creatures are not to be owned. Man can keep them captive or bribe them through their hunger, but he cannot own them. Only if they are loved they may stay with him as friends."

"You grow old, Magus," said the King, "and you talk an old man's folly. Tomorrow we shall search the whole forest."

All next day men hunted for the silver colt until, as the last light was fading, they glimpsed him drinking at a stream. Very softly, very quietly, the circle of hunters closed upon him. Skillfully the head groom flung his coil of rope, and the noose fell neatly over the colt's head and tightened as he reared. Others ran to help him and they dragged the terrified colt up the bank. As he reached the top, he stopped kicking and stood quite still while the men drew near.

He was shivering and flecked with foam, and dark patches of sweat stained his shining flanks. Nearer came the head groom and nearer, with gentle soothing sounds. He was almost near enough to touch him and still the colt made no move. Then, as the man reached out his hand, he gave a high whinnying call, plunged, and reared again like a fountain of silver fire. The strong rope snapped like a piece of string, he had burst through the ring of his enemies with a stallion's anger and pride, and the twilight closed on the thunder of his hooves.

The King was furious when he heard what had happened.

"Fools!" he stormed. "Fools, to trust only to a rope. Go again tomorrow. The snow is thicker and food in the forest must be scarce. Build a high, strong, fenced enclosure near his drinking place, hide the entrance with branches, and bait it with good fresh hay. Hunger will bring him in."

The hunters did just as he had said. The fence was of strong logs, nine feet high, and the entrance skillfully hidden. All day they waited, until darkness came and the moon rose. Then, moving softly as a deer, the silver colt slipped out between the trees and down to the stream to drink. As he climbed the bank again and blew the drops of water from his muzzle, the sweet scent of the hay floated to him. He sniffed it and waited and sniffed again. But he smelled no danger and he came closer and closer to the hidden entrance. As he reached it and began to eat, the hunters leaped out, driving him forward, and dropped the heavy entrance bar into place behind him.

"Safe at last!" said the chief huntsman. "His Majesty will be satisfied this time."

But after his first frightened plunge, the captive was trotting round and round the trap they had made, searching for an escape. Finding none, he reared, his mane and tail streaming like water in the moonlight, and he screamed with rage and fierce disdain. Again he reared and plunged, then with two great galloping strides he gathered every steel-coiled muscle and leaped as if for the stars. He was over the fence as if it was no more than a field hedge, and away and lost in the dark.

"It isn't possible!" roared the King. "No horse could leap that height. There must have been a gap in the fence."

"Sire," said Magus, "did I not tell you that this colt must run free? He is a prince among his own kind, as you are a king among yours."

"When he is broken and reined and ridden, he shall be the prince of my whole stable," retorted the King. "Use your ancient knowledge to better purpose, Magus, and tell me how I can catch him."

"Majesty, you will never do so. Only one thing will hold him—a net that will catch the wind."

"I have never heard of such a net," said the King.

But he set every weaver and spinner in the kingdom to work. They made nets of silk, of gossamer, of gold and silver thread, of thistledown woven in thousandfold thickness. But none of them could hold or catch the wind.

With each disappointment the King's desire grew, until it began to eat away his heart and make him cruel. Once again he sent for Magus.

"Old man," he said dangerously, "you have tried to cheat me. There is no such thing as a net to catch the wind. Tell me the truth this time or you shall lie in prison to the end of your days."

Magus was indeed old and frail and he feared the King's anger. He spoke slowly and unwillingly.

"Sire, I have told you the truth, though you do not understand it. But I have read in old books that there is another way."

"What other way?"

"Do not ask me, Your Majesty. Do not use it. It will end only in grief and loss."

"What other way?" insisted the King.

"It is said that the rare ones, such as he, will come willingly to a young and gentle girl who loves them, and will even rest beside her."

"Mirabelle!"

"Do not ask her. Do not make her choose between obedience to her father and her love for the silver colt."

The King smiled thinly. "She will not have to choose."

He sent at once for his daughter and talked to her with much kindness.

"The colt must run free, Mirabelle. There is no net that will catch the wind."

"I am so glad, Father. I knew you would understand at last."

The King sighed. "I meant only to honor him, to let him be seen and admired as he should be. No one but the King himself would ever have ridden him. But now I fear he may have left the forest, for he has not been seen for many days."

"Let me look for him, Father. Perhaps he would not be afraid of me."

"Do so indeed, my child, and tell me where you find him. Take sugar and apples with you to show that you mean him no harm."

Happily Mirabelle set off. The snow had long since melted, the thrusting grass was speckled with early flowers, and the trees were full of birdsong. And there, in the glade where she had first seen him, she found the silver colt. He was grazing quietly alone in the sunlight, but lifted his head at her soft call.

She set down the bag of apples the King had given her from his own table, and held one out on the palm of her hand. His pricked ears heard the love in her voice and he answered with a soft whicker of delight. Gentle, inquiring, foot by delicate foot, he began to move toward her. He reached out his head and took the apple, while she ran her hand along the arch of his neck. She saw that his color was changing as he grew. His coat was turning to the creamy whiteness of May blossoms, and his mane and tail glimmered as pale as starlight.

"Starlight!" she whispered to him. "That's what I'll call you. Starlight!"

He nuzzled her shoulder as if he understood, and she gave him a second apple. With a sigh he folded his slender forelegs and lay down among the flowers, and Mirabelle sat beside him stroking his head. At first she thought he only wanted rest. Then she saw how still he was and how slowly he breathed, and she was gripped with sudden fear.

"Starlight! What is it? What is it? Oh, Starlight, you can't *die*!"

Her father's grooms stepped out from the trees behind her.

"Have no fear, Princess. The colt is only asleep. There was a potion in the apples that you gave him. We are here to take him to the King."

Mirabelle sprang up, crying out with grief and horror.

"No, no! You mustn't touch him. My father said he should run free."

"Free until he could be caught," said the chief groom.

All her cries and struggles were useless. They lifted the colt onto a litter and carried him back to the palace, and Mirabelle wept all the way as she followed.

As they passed through the stable courtyard the other horses threw up their heads and whinnied and trampled in their stalls as if they caught the sense of danger or excitement. But the yearling never moved, not even when they laid him down in the stable prepared for him. It was unlike the others. It was spacious and warm, but it had thick stone walls and iron doors that not even he could leap or break.

Mirabelle ran to find her father.

"Father, how could you? You have made me betray him! You have broken your own promise! He will never trust anyone again."

"Hush, child. You talk foolishly. When he is full grown no king in the world will have a horse like him. He shall be treated like a prince. He will learn to live here like the others and be happy."

"He will never be happy without his freedom," mourned Mirabelle. "Nor can I ever love you again while you hold him a prisoner."

"You will both come to your senses," said the King.

He left her and went down to the stables to rejoice in his prize. But the colt would not let him, nor any man, come near. He screamed with rage, and kicked and plunged, his dark eyes flashing angry fire, and no one dared approach him. At last, fearing the colt would hurt himself, the King sent for his daughter.

At the sound of her voice the colt became quiet, and she slipped into his stall through a narrow little door from the palace itself. It was the only entrance they dared to use until their captive was tamed. She ran to him, weeping bitterly, and clasped her arms about his neck.

"Oh, Starlight! Starlight! I didn't know! I'd never have betrayed you. Will you ever forgive me?"

The colt rubbed his beautiful head against her, while real tears ran down his velvet nose, as if he understood and shared her grief.

"They will both get over it," said the King.

But he was wrong. The colt had spent his anger, but he drooped and pined. His eyes lost their luster and his once shining coat grew dull. Mirabelle became day by day thinner and more silent, and a shadow seemed to lie over the palace.

Unable to sleep, the Princess leaned from her window one

night when the moon was full. The white flowers in the garden below her glimmered as Starlight's coat had done when he was free. She could bear it no longer. She dressed and crept out through the sleeping rooms of the palace and along its dim corridors, down and down to a little door that opened into the garden. Two great dogs guarded it, but they knew her and only wagged their tails in greeting as she passed.

From the gardens it was easy to reach the stables. The iron doors of Starlight's stall had never yet been opened. It took all her strength to draw the huge bolts that held them. Her hands were torn and bleeding when at last she dragged open the doors. Moonlight flooded in, turning the straw to silver heaps and glittering in the dark eyes of the colt. He was waiting for her, poised and still, his head at last proudly lifted. His whicker of love was so low it could hardly be heard, but he breathed sweetly against her as she threw her arms round him and rubbed her face against his neck.

"Good-bye, my darling! Go now! Go quickly!"

He trotted out into the yard, quietly on his unshod hooves, like a bright reflection of the moon itself. The other horses stirred and shifted in their stalls as he passed, but made no other sound. It seemed as if they knew but would not betray him. Under the courtyard archway he stopped, and turned his head in a gesture of farewell. Then she heard the muffled drumming of his hooves as he flung into a gallop, heading for the forest like a shooting star.

There was no return for either of them now. Her father's anger would be terrible against her. With a glad but aching heart she watched the colt go. Then she drew her cloak around her and followed him, a small sad shadow fading into the dark.

The King's anger was terrible indeed when he found both the colt and his daughter gone. He sent out huntsmen to search the forest, companies of soldiers to seek and arrest the Princess, messengers to every part of the kingdom to search for news. But days drew into weeks and still nothing was heard of either of the runaways. The King's anger began to ebb into despair. Every day he himself rode in the forest, escaping from his lonely, empty palace. But he could not escape from himself. Sometimes he would sit a long time, lost in his own dark thoughts, in the glade where the colt had first been seen.

Waiting there one day, he was roused by the gentle rub of a horse's nose against his shoulder. He sprang up, full of hope. But it was only his own horse, Thunder, who had once been his favorite. Thunder could not understand or bear his master's sadness, but gave him the only comfort that he could. And suddenly the mist of anger and disappointment cleared from the King's brain, and he looked with new eyes at his horse.

"Thunder! How could I forget you, my beauty, my pride? Yet still you are faithful to me. Forgive me, my friend."

He clapped his hand against the black column of the horse's neck, and the creature pricked up his ears and gave a little dancing step of joy to feel himself caressed as he used to be. Desire had eaten the King's heart away till it was as small as a dry nut, but in that moment it began to grow once more.

Back in the palace he sent for Magus.

"Magus, old friend, I should have listened to you long ago. My folly and desire have indeed brought grief and loss just as you warned me. I am wise too late. Tell me, is there any hope?"

"There is always hope, Your Majesty. If word reaches the Princess that she need not fear, perhaps she will return."

The King recalled all his soldiers and sent a proclamation to every town and village, that the return of the Princess Mirabelle would be a day of public rejoicing. But still there was no sign of her, and the palace seemed every day more lonely and more silent.

Then the King made another proclamation, that anyone who could bring the Princess home would have half the royal treasury as a reward. Day after day sentries paced the palace walls, looking for some messenger, and heralds waited to announce his arrival. But none ever came.

It was high summer again. The King sat alone in his great hall, heartsick and weary. Suddenly a trumpet sounded, clear and shrill, from the outer walls. It was answered by another and another. A messenger at last!

Wild with hope he hurried to the palace gates, unable to wait for news. Courtiers and servants thronged there too.

Someone was riding down the road from the forest. A girl with her long hair flowing free, a girl on a white horse.

A great sigh of joy went rippling through the crowd like wind through a cornfield.

"Mirabelle!" The King would have run to meet her. But now the girl and her horse were close enough to be clearly seen, and a sudden hush fell upon all who watched. Astonishment and awe held them silent. For this was no horse of ordinary kind. His coat was as shining white as cherry blossoms in spring, his silver hooves seemed hardly to touch the ground. His mane and tail glittered like a waterfall in starlight. And from the center of his forehead sprang a single gleaming silver horn. Without saddle or bridle, he was free as the wind. He was full of pride and fire and grace, and carried the Princess in willing courtesy, not in bondage.

"The unicorn!" whispered Magus. "The magical unicorn! I half knew it yet dared not hope."

"You knew it? The silver colt?"

But Mirabelle had slipped down from the unicorn's back and was running to her father.

"Father! Oh, Father, I have missed you so much. Can you forgive me?"

The King caught and held her, and all the months of sorrow fell away.

"It is I who need forgiveness," he said humbly. "My dearest child, where have you been and how have you lived all this while?"

"Starlight took care of me. He carried me away into a far country until he was full grown and we knew it was safe to return."

Her father bowed his head to the unicorn as if he too were a reigning king.

"My lord, I have done you great wrong and insult, and you have repaid me with great good. How can I make amends?"

Magus laughed with happiness. "He will not want the promised half of your treasury, Sire."

But Mirabelle had laid her cheek against the unicorn's and listened as if he spoke to her. Then she turned to the King.

"There is one thing he desires. A great thing, if you will give it."

"If it is in my power, the gift is his."

"He wishes that all the horses in your stables may be set free to go where they will."

The King's heart nearly failed him. To lose them all, his splendid horses, his greatest pride and joy! But he had given a promise and this time he would not betray it. Sadly he gave the command.

They were led out into the sunlight, tossing their heads and dancing with delight—black and bay and chestnut and white, every one of them magnificent. And each, as he saw the unicorn, bowed his head as if to a prince.

"Free them!" commanded the King.

The grooms slipped off the bridles, and at once the whole herd streamed away over the summer grass, a foaming river of floating manes and tails and flashing hooves, exulting to be free. Some galloped straight on and were lost to sight among the forest trees. But others checked and swerved and cantered back, whickering as they came. All the King's loved favorites—Thunder and Jasmine and Blood Royal and many more—were jostling together for his caresses. Some went straight to their own grooms. The most elegant white mare of the whole herd nuzzled against the youngest stable boy, who threw his arms about her neck and kissed her in his joy at her return.

The King looked round at all of them, light of heart as he had never been before.

"They have chosen," he said. "Let each man keep the horse that loves him best."

The unicorn bent his lovely head, lowering his horn as if in salute. Then he too turned and whirled away, galloping toward the forest. They watched as he grew smaller in the distance, a moon, a star, a spark of pure white light that vanished all at once in the dense shade of the trees.

The King gave a long sigh. "Will he ever come back again?"

"He will come back," promised Mirabelle. "Whenever he wishes, he will come back."

"He will come back," echoed Magus. "For the Princess has caught him, Sire, as you have caught these horses. She has caught him with love, the net that will catch the wind."

115369

DATE DUE

J
G
Greaves, Margaret
A net to catch the wind.